FOR MY FRIENDS

First published in the United States, Great Britain, Canada, Australia, and New Zealand in 2001
by NorthSouth Books, Inc., an imprint of NordSüd Verlag AG, CH-8005 Zürich, Switzerland.

This edition published in 2015 by NorthSouth Books, Inc.,
an imprint of NordSüd Verlag AG, CH-8005 Zürich, Switzerland.

Library of Congress Cataloging-in-Publication Data is available.

The CIP catalogue record for this book is available from The British Library.

ISBN: 978-0-7358-4211-3

Printed in China by Leo Paper Products Ltd., Heshan, Guangdong, January 2015.

1 3 5 7 9 · 10 8 6 4 2

www.northsouth.com

Goldilocks
and the Three Bears

Retold and illustrated by
Valeri Gorbachev

North
South

O nce upon a time, there were three bears who lived together in a little cottage in the woods. There was a great big father bear, a middle-sized mother bear, and a wee small baby bear.

One morning the three bears decided to go for a walk
in the woods while their breakfast porridge cooled.

While they were gone, a little girl named Goldilocks came past their cottage.

She peeked in the window, and when she saw that no one was at home, she went inside.

There on the table sat the three bowls of porridge. The porridge smelled so delicious that Goldilocks just had to have some.

First she tried the porridge in the great big father bear's great big bowl, but it was too hot.

Next she tried the porridge in the middle-sized mother bear's middle-sized bowl, but it was too cold.

Then she tried the porridge in the wee small baby bear's wee small bowl, and it was just right! So she ate it all up.

When she had finished the porridge, Goldilocks wandered into the sitting room, where she found the three bears' chairs.

First she tried the great big father bear's great big chair, but it was too hard.

Next she tried the middle-sized mother bear's middle-sized chair, but it was too soft.

Then she tried the wee small baby bear's wee small chair, and it was just right! So Goldilocks sat down in the chair . . .

and broke it all to bits!

Then Goldilocks went upstairs, where she found the three bears' beds.

First she tried the great big father bear's great big bed, but it was too hard.

Next she tried the middle-sized mother bear's middle-sized bed, but it was too soft.

Then she tried the wee small baby bear's wee small
bed, and it was just right! So Goldilocks lay down and
fell fast asleep.

No sooner had Goldilocks fallen asleep
than the three bears returned home.
Their walk had made them very hungry,
so they hurried right into the kitchen.

Goldilocks had left the spoon in the great big father bear's porridge.

"Someone has been eating my porridge!" said the great big father bear in his great big voice.

The middle-sized mother bear saw that the spoon had been left in her bowl of porridge, too. "Someone has been eating my porridge!" said the middle-sized mother bear in her middle-sized voice.

Then the wee small baby bear looked at his bowl of porridge. "Someone has been eating my porridge!" cried the wee small baby bear in his wee small voice. "And they've eaten it all up!"

The three bears hurried into the sitting room.

Goldilocks had knocked the pillow off the great big father bear's chair. "Someone has been sitting in my chair!" said the great big father bear in his great big voice.

The pillow on the middle-sized mother bear's chair had been moved, too. "Someone has been sitting in my chair!" said the middle-sized mother bear in her middle-sized voice.

Then the wee small baby bear looked at his chair.

"Someone has been sitting in my chair," cried the wee small baby bear in his wee small voice, "and they've broken it to bits!"

Then the three bears went upstairs.

Goldilocks had messed up the covers on the great big father bear's bed.

"Someone has been sleeping in my bed!" said the great big father bear in his great big voice.

The covers on the middle-sized mother bear's bed had been messed up, too.

"Someone has been sleeping in my bed!" said the middle-sized mother bear in her middle-sized voice.

Then the wee small baby bear
looked at his bed.

"Someone has been sleeping in my bed!"
cried the wee small baby bear in his wee small voice.
"And here she is!"
 Goldilocks woke with a start.

She leaped out of bed, jumped through the window, clambered down from the roof, and ran away just as fast as she could go.

What happened to Goldilocks afterward, no one knows. The three bears never saw her again, and they lived happily ever after in their cottage in the woods.